The
Splendid
Splinter

a novel for all ages

ALSO BY LEE SILBER

Sunshine

The Homeless Hero

Runaway Best Seller

Summer Stories

Show And Tell Organizing

No Brown M&Ms!

The Ripple Effect

Creative Careers

Bored Games

The Wild Idea Club

Rock To Riches

Chicken Soup For The Beach Lover's Soul (Contributor)

Organizing From The Right Side Of The Brain

Money Management For The Creative Person

Self-Promotion For The Creative Person

Career Management For The Creative Person

Time Management For The Creative Person

Aim First

Notes, Quotes & Advice

Successful San Diegans

Dating in San Diego

The
Splendid
Splinter

A novel

LEE SILBER

THE SPLENDID SPLINTER

Lee Silber

Deep Impact Publishing
822 Redondo Court
San Diego CA 92109

To buy copies of this book in bulk, inquire about having the author appear at your book club or speak to your group, or just for more information in general, please contact the author at:
www.leesilber.com, 858-735-4533, leesilber@leesilber.com

Cover Design: Lee Silber
Interior Design: Lee Silber

First Printing June 2018

This is a work of fiction. All the names, characters, and places are either invented or used fictitiously. The exceptions are the real people or places used with permission.

Retail Price: $10.00

*To all those at the Islandia Marina who called
my late father a friend, thank you.*

—LEE SILBER

*"When I walk down the street I want people to say,
'There goes Ted Williams, the greatest hitter who ever lived.'"*

—TED WILLIAMS

CHAPTER ONE

Absorbing the bone-jarring explosion from below, Doc suddenly realized it was only a matter of minutes before he would drown. His beloved fifty-four-foot Bertram cabin cruiser was already listed to port, and Doc frantically struggled to free his hands, tightly taped behind his back. The two goons had also done a very professional job of taping his ankles together, securing them to the base of the captain's chair bolted to the salon floor. As the boat continued to lean to the left, Doc was suspended in the chair—a chair he had sat in thousands of times, but never at this odd angle. He watched as ocean water rushed in through the hole in the window... a bullet hole.

After being beaten and tortured for nearly four hours, it was hard to focus. He knew he needed to concentrate on finding a way out of this mess, but he kept drifting in and out of consciousness, and he hurt all over. Doc wasn't sure if his vision was blurred from having his glasses knocked off or from the repeated blows to his head and face that had left one eye swollen shut. Since his blood was splattered everywhere, he guessed it was the beating that made it hard for him to think and see. Always a fighter, Doc was coming to the realization this may be a fight he wouldn't be able to win. A wave of hopelessness overwhelmed him, and his world faded to black.

Moments later, Doc was jolted awake. Pictures and mementos were falling all around him as the bow of *The Splendid Splinter* started to slip into the sea. It was like a last gasp for the boat as it started heading to its final resting place at the bottom of the ocean. Reluctantly ready to accept his own fate as well, Doc noticed a picture that had dropped into his lap as the boat angled to its grave. It was the 1980 Padres team photo. In the back row, Doc stood shoulder to shoulder with the other coaches. This brought a smile to his face. He had never married, never had kids. Baseball was his first and only love. He had no regrets. He scanned the photo with his good eye and found Taylor James, the rookie Doc had taken under his wing and taught how to hit a curve, and how to be a man. Thinking about Taylor gave him a warm feeling.

The rising water level in the old boat quickly replaced any warm, fuzzy feelings he had. The frigid water was up to his knees now. As calm a man as you could ever meet, Doc was beginning to panic. He frantically scanned the salon looking for anything that would buy him some time, or save his life. The sunrise cast a glow in the cabin that allowed him to see, the light lifted his spirits. Doc did his best to push down the alarm and anxiety welling inside him so he could think clearly and rationally. To calm down, Doc closed his eyes and visualized the surroundings he had called home for the past twenty years. He moved through the boat in his mind. Try as he might, he couldn't come up with any way to free himself.

As the ocean water continued to rise, up to his chest now,

he knew he didn't have much time. He struggled against the tape that bound his hands and feet, but the harder he fought, the tighter the tape seemed to get. Instead, he used his weight to move the top half of chair around, stopping to rest, his head pounding as though men with jackhammers were in his skull working away. By now, the boat was nearly at a 90 degree angle and minutes away from plunging to the bottom. He made a quick decision. There wasn't enough time to save himself, but he might be able to get a distress call out and at least let someone know where he went down.

He swung the chair around until he saw his hand-held VHF radio, still lodged against the instrument console. If his hands were free, he could just reach out and make that mayday call. Now he had to crane his neck just to breathe. The bone-chilling water engulfed him and he was numb from the neck down. As the boat arched and began its final descent, something fell and hit him on the head. Doc reached up to rub the bump and realized that his hand was free. The cold water had caused his skin to shrink and he unconsciously slipped his hand out of the tape.

He reached for the radio and tried to turn it on, but his hands were so cold and unresponsive he couldn't even turn the knob! The radio was waterproof, so he knew it would work, if he could work it. So he used his teeth. "Hurry," he thought. Fortunately, these types of radios are preset to channel 16, the emergency frequency. He was barely able to squeeze the "send" button and found it even harder to talk, but he managed to croak out, "Mayday, mayday, this is *The*

Splendid Splinter and I'm sinking fast...."

The last of the transmission was garbled, since Doc could no longer get his head above water to speak. He had expelled all of his air to yell into the radio and now he was completely underwater, cut off from any air. It wasn't long before he lost consciousness, but not before he gave it his all, just like he had taught his players. His last fleeting thoughts were of his good friend and baseball legend, Yogi Berra, "It ain't over 'til it's over."

He knew it was over, but he held down the transmit button until his lungs filled with water and he slipped away.

CHAPTER TWO

The same sunrise that was Doc's last warmed the now quiet Island Marina, tucked into a cozy corner of San Diego's Mission Bay. There was the usual dawn activity—the charter boat crews beginning their preparations for another summer's day of booming business from the "Zonies" who came to San Diego to escape the Arizona heat; Then there was Harry, the boat cleaner, who began the daily routine of getting his gear together, before slipping into the water to scrape the incessant and resilient barnacles from the bottoms of the boats. A few bleary-eyed tourists, who were staying at the nearby Hyatt, wandered about in the early morning light in search of a cup of coffee, obviously still operating on East Coast time. Generally, the live-a-boards weren't seen or heard from until later in the morning as they made their daily pilgrimage to the marina's showers and bathrooms. Except for Christine Hollingsworth.

The pretty physical education teacher and former Olympic volleyball player was hard to miss, as she sat stretched her fit six-foot-two athletic frame on the grass next to the dock master's office. Christie wore a skintight running outfit that showed off her perfect physique. Her long blonde hair was pulled back into a ponytail and stuffed into a Padres cap. Her daily routine was a five-mile run, followed by a one-mile ocean swim, before she headed off to enrich the lives of San Diego's inner-city youths. Nine months a year, five days a week, plus tournaments on every other weekend—that was Christie's life. She was looking forward to some time off. Summer break hadn't come a moment too soon.

"Hi, Christie," Les, the Dock Master said with a smile as he looked down at her stretching on the grass. "How are you this fine morning?"

"Better. Much better," Christie said enthusiastically as she looked up.

"You're in an especially good mood today."

"I know. I finished grading papers and I cleaned out my classroom yesterday, so I'm on vacation. Thank God."

"Good for you. I wish I only had to work nine months a year." He shrugged. "But this is the busy season for me, as you know, so I'd better get to work. Say, 'hello' to your dad for me." Les waved good-bye and headed for his tiny office overlooking the marina.

"I will. See ya later, Les," Christie called after him, as she ran in the opposite direction.

Christie used her run to rewind the year. She loved her job and the kids loved her. She had led the women's volleyball team to another winning season and helped three of her girls get college scholarships—no small feat, considering their grades. She was clearly the favorite teacher at San Diego High.

But it had also been a trying year. A teacher had been

seriously wounded in a school shooting, and many of her students had either dropped out or were incarcerated. After two years of teaching gang-bangers and crackheads, she had applied for and landed a new cushy position at La Jolla High School in the fall. Not only was she moving to a better school, and the bump in salary wouldn't hurt either.

Christie felt cramped living aboard her 38-foot Beneteau sailboat and wanted to move into a real home. She'd looked forward to not having to stoop all the time and living somewhere that wasn't damp every day. Someday, she would like to settle down, get married, start a family, and live in a house, although at her age she wasn't in any real hurry. The problem was, the man she loved since she was a teenager had no idea how she felt. He was much older and thought of her as a child. She had to tell him how she felt and show him that she wasn't that tall and gangly teenager anymore, she was all grown up.

As she ran past Dog Beach and turned around to head back she decided that this summer would be a transition point in her life. She had to tell the love of her life she was saving herself for him. Not that it had been hard to do. She loved him with all her heart, and all the other men she met paled in comparison. Besides, being so tall, athletic, and beautiful, she tended to intimidate men. As Christie ran past Marina Village, the site of many outdoor weddings, she made up her mind. It was time to tell her future husband how she felt.

She stopped suddenly as she came to an empty slip. Doc's boat was missing. It had been there, day and night, rain and shine, for at least the past two years. Now it was gone. Her feeling of surprise was replaced by a vague sense of unease. Doc hadn't said a word about going anywhere. But while he might not have told her, he usually shared his plans with Taylor. Maybe Taylor would know where Doc had gone. A second item to add to her list of what she wanted to tell him.

CHAPTER THREE

Christie bent over Taylor's bunk. He was lying on his back, lightly snoring and dressed in the outfit he had come home in. She shook him gently. "Taylor, wake up," Christie whispered. "Taylor. Come on, I need to talk to you." When he didn't respond, she raised her voice. "Taylor, please wake-up."

"Jeez, I can't believe this," she said to herself. She moved from the foot of his bed in the forward berth of Taylor's boat and climbed up on top of him as he slept soundly.

She shook him and yelled, "Taylor James, get your lazy butt up right now! Right now!"

Bam. Taylor shot straight up and hit his skull on the bulkhead. As he rubbed the knot developing on his head he angrily screamed, "What? WHAT?"

Christie blurted out, "Doc's boat is missing."

With half-open eyes, Taylor groggily tried to grasp what he had heard before responding. "First of all, could you please move your sweaty body off me so I can get up?" Forgetting she had straddled his chest to shake him awake, Christie slid off to one side.

"Thanks," Taylor said as he sat up. "Do you have any idea what time it is?" He asked, pointing at his wall clock. "Not everyone is a morning person like you."

Christie glanced over her shoulder. "8:30, so what?"

"Do you have any idea what time I got in last night?" Taylor asked.

"Did you have a hot date or something?" Christie asked snidely, not really wanting to know the answer.

"No," he said rather testily. "It was my reserve weekend and I was on a...." Taylor stopping himself before revealing the nature of his assignment. The truth was, he was a weekend warrior attached to the mobile diving salvage unit (MDSU) stationed at North Island. Usually his unit just dressed up and played soldier one weekend a month and two weeks each summer. But this weekend was different. He and the guys took part in a joint exercise with the SEALs.

"Oh" was all Christie could say, but she couldn't control the grin that spread across her face. She quickly caught herself and concern returned to her face. "Taylor, did you hear me? Doc's boat is gone."

"That's impossible. Doc's boat hasn't moved in years. I don't even think he remembers how to start it."

"I know, Taylor, that's why I'm so worried."

"Maybe he's having it hauled out to have the bottom painted," but Taylor knew Doc would have told him if he was having that done.

Christie knew that, too. "Did he tell you he was having the bottom painted?"

"No, he didn't."

"Don't you think it's odd he didn't tell you he was going

somewhere?" Christie asked.

Taylor ran his hands through his hair and nodded. It was true. Ever since his rookie year with the Padres when Doc was the hitting instructor, the two had become inseparable. Doc was his best friend, father figure, and neighbor all rolled into one. It was Doc who encouraged Taylor to buy a boat when he signed a big contract extension. As Doc put it, "No matter what happens, you'll always have a place to live."

He was right. After two and a half outstanding years with the Padres, Taylor had permanently damaged his shoulder when he smashed into the wall at The Murph. He tried to come back with the Mets and Pirates, but the injury was too severe. He would always be known as the Padres right-fielder before Tony Gwynn and after Dave Winfield... the guy nobody could remember. Fortunately, he had contract guarantees that paid him enough to buy the boat and start a savings account.

"Well?" Christie said trying to snap Taylor out of his trip down memory lane.

"Well, what?"

"When was the last time you talked to Doc? Did he say anything about having his boat worked on or taking it out?"

Feeling a little guilty since Doc's boat was directly across from his and he hadn't talked to him in a week.

Taylor hung his head. "You know how Doc and I have our morning ritual of going over the box scores and analyzing the Padres game?"

"Yes."

"Well, I've been kinda busy lately and I haven't been over to see him in over a week."

"Taylor, hanging out with you is what Doc lives for. That and baseball."

"I know, I know. I'll make it up to him when I see him."

"That's just it. Where is he? I'm really worried."

"Yeah. I'm sure there is some perfectly logical explanation why Doc and *The Splendid Splinter* are gone. Let me get cleaned up and we'll go ask around and see if anyone knows what's going on."

"I already talked to Les this morning and he didn't know anything. We should talk to Ann-Marie."

Ann-Marie worked at the Island Cantina attached to the marina. If anything happened in the marina, Ann-Marie knew about it—sometimes even before it actually happened. Ann-Marie was more than a waitress. She was an unofficial marriage counselor, business advisor, baby sitter and, most of all, a friend to the boaters. As Taylor rubbed his eyes and noticed a black substance on his fingers, Christie asked, "Taylor, what is that dark stuff smeared on your face?"

"Oh, yeah, when I got home from my reserve weekend exercises I was so tired I must have just fallen into bed and passed out."

No matter how close he and Christie were, he wasn't supposed to talk about the nature of his classified work with the Navy. Christie thought he just went away and fooled around, but his unit actually did some fairly dangerous and covert work from time to time—then they fooled around.

"I'll just be a minute. Let me shower and shave." He got up, still wearing his Navy issue shorts, gray T-shirt and boots.

"Do you always sleep in your clothes?" Christie asked.

Taylor raised an eyebrow and flashed a big grin, showing off his dimples and rugged good looks, and winked. Taylor stared at Christie and then gestured with his hand as if to say, "Do you mind?" and waited for her to turn around before he pulled off his tee and shorts and headed for the shower. Christie couldn't help but sneak a peek as he went by.

"Get a grip," she thought to herself. Whenever she was around Taylor, she acted like a schoolgirl in love for the first time. Funny thing was, that is exactly how it had always been between them. When they first met, she was a school girl. She remembered thinking at the time it was love at first sight—for her.

She stretched her slender frame on his bed and buried her head in his pillow and screamed. If only he would pick up on her signals. She wasn't a teenager anymore, but a woman who loved him. When they first met she was only fourteen. At the time all she was interested in was volleyball. Her freakish height gave her a tremendous advantage in sports, but was a hindrance when it came to boys. All that changed when her father's best friend, Doc Skinner, brought the starting right-fielder for the San Diego Padres over for dinner. From the moment Christie met the strapping Taylor James, she was smitten. Christie wasn't interested in boys any longer. She was enamored with a man ten years her senior, but in a semi-innocent way.

CHAPTER FOUR

Christie's father was a big baseball fan and he and Taylor became fast friends. Taylor was at their house in the Coronado
Cays all the time. Sometimes she and Taylor would play beach
volleyball at the Strand across the road or shoot hoops at the
park. Her favorite times were when Taylor gave her a ride on
his motorcycle into the Coronado village where they would
get ice cream and sit on the grass and talk about sports.

She let her mind wander back to those angst-filled days
as she lay there smelling his scent on the pillow and remi-
niscing about how she had made every effort to get Taylor
to notice her. But Taylor never touched her. The fact that she
was a teenager and her father the Chief of Police on Coronado
Island may have had something to do with that.

So Christie became a baseball fanatic—make that a
Taylor James fanatic. Her room was plastered with his pictures, jersey, and other memorabilia. The first thing she did
each morning was check the box score to see how her "boy-
friend" had done. Her father didn't seem to mind. He figured
the young man was smart enough not to make a move on an
innocent kid, even if she did look like a model. Christie later
found out that Taylor was exactly the kind of man The Chief

hoped she would meet and marry some day—just not for a very long time.

Taylor would occasionally call her from the road, and on some nights they would talk baseball for hours. Since Christie didn't have a social life to speak of, her calls from Taylor were the highlight of her week. She knew he saw her as a friend, but she couldn't help how she felt—she was deeply in love with him. In the summer she attended all of his games. She had nothing else to do and it kept her mind off things like the death of her mother who had passed away when Christie was eleven. She knew Taylor pitied her, but she liked the attention. Her father was always at work and Christie was usually left alone, so when Taylor was in town, he would offer to take her to the movies and out to eat.

Then, when Taylor hurt his shoulder, he grew distant and angry. When he couldn't come back, he retired from baseball and joined the Navy. He was stationed in Hawaii. The two of them didn't see each other very often. There was a tension between them that wasn't there before. The tables had turned. Now she was the star athlete, and college scholarships were flowing in from all over the country for her to be a part of their volleyball program. She chose UC Santa Barbara for their volleyball program and Christie dominated at the collegiate level. She was so good she was chosen to be on the women's Olympic Volleyball Team. When she blew out a knee, it was Taylor who was there to help her heal. She never did make it to the Olympics.

Afterward, she came home to teach. As a graduation

present, her father bought her a sailboat. She moved it to the Island Marina to be closer to Taylor's boat and Taylor. Her boat was badly in need of some TLC, and the first day she was there Taylor came by her slip with sandwiches in one hand and a sander in the other. She fell in love with him all over again that summer. That was more than two years ago.

"Hey, Christie, I'll meet you on your boat in ten minutes," Taylor yelled from the shower. She didn't reply, or move. She hoped to catch him coming out of the shower. Who knows? She lay back in the bed, pretending to read a copy of Baseball Weekly. When she heard the water shut off, she chickened out and went to the galley to make some coffee. "Jeez, what a mess," she thought to herself. "Taylor needs someone to look after him, whether he knows it or not."

Taylor came into the galley wearing only a pair of trunks and a hat. He took the cup of coffee Christie handed him. She looked into his eyes and saw concern—something the usually upbeat Taylor didn't show. Christie looked him up and down and felt a stirring in her heart. Taylor stood well over six-feet tall, muscular, but in a lean, athletic way. He had a deep tan for early summer and his curly blonde hair was cropped short on the sides for his Navy reserve weekend. Taylor took a sip of his coffee and went topside to see Doc's missing boat for himself. Christie followed him up, and they both just stood there staring at the empty slip.

CHAPTER FIVE

Taylor's mind raced with the possibilities, none of them good. He was also feeling guilty about not spending enough time with Doc lately. He took a swig of his coffee and poured the rest in the water beside his boat. He set the cup down on the lock box and started to untie his dinghy.

"Christy, try to call Ann-Marie," Taylor said as he handed her his phone.

After letting it ring ten times Christie hung up.

"No answer?"

"Nope."

"I bet she's there. She probably just unplugged the phone so she could sleep in. We'll take my dinghy, it'll be faster than driving." It was true. Most of the errands they needed to run were quicker by boat. Need a part for your boat? Motor across the marina to Bill's Boat Supply. Want to watch *Monday Night Football*? It's a short dinghy ride to the Pennant. Need a snack? There are several eateries where you can park your boat and grab a bite. Ann-Marie lived on the bay side of Mission Beach in a cute little yellow cottage she shared with her young son. She was a single mom struggling to make it by waitressing as many shifts as she could handle.

The Island Cantina was a rare place where boaters and tourists co-existed. Ann-Marie was good with both crowds. The cantina sat on stilts and overlooked the marina, which connected to two large hotels full of conventioneers. It was quite a spectacle to watch the two decidedly different types mix and mingle. The boaters dressed casually in dock shoes, shorts, and aloha shirts; the conventioneers in their suits and ties. The conventioneers sat at the bar and drooled looking out at all the boats and dreamed of someday chucking it all to live on a boat. The live-aboards just drooled.

Taylor sometimes would sit at the bar and listen to the business travelers brag about their stock options, fancy cars, and big homes and feel a twinge of jealousy. He wondered if he should take a run at a real job. Taylor had tried his hand at sales, dabbled in real estate, and worked as a boat cleaner for a while, but none of these things really interested him.

As a player, he had made decent money, nothing like today's athletes, but enough to buy a boat, at least. He had his pension from Major League Baseball, his Navy reserve paychecks, and the occasional odd job here and there. It was enough to live comfortably by himself. But before he could settle down with someone else, he knew he would need more stability in his life. To settle down he needed the right girl and the right girl didn't want a washed-up baseball player with no real prospects for prosperity. Or so he thought.

CHAPTER SIX

After Taylor started the little outboard, Christie expertly cast off and hopped in the dinghy. When Taylor turned the dinghy in the opposite direction from Ann-Marie's, Christie yelled over the sound of the motor, "Where are we going?"

"Let's pass by the boatyard and see if Doc's boat has been hauled out," Taylor said, knowing it was an exercise in futility, but working closely with the Navy SEALs had taught him to be thorough.

"Didn't you talk to Doc before you left to go pretend you are G.I. Joe?" Christie asked.

"Yeah, and I let him hold my toy gun and apply my face paint."

"Funny, being a boat away I would have thought you would have talked to him before you left."

"What about you? You pass by his boat every day. When is the last time you talked to him?" They both hung their heads.

"I'm usually in a rush to get to school in the mornings and I just wave and keep going. At night I've got papers to grade."

"Don't be so hard on yourself. I've been busy coaching that bunch of brats up at the private school up the hill."

"Taylor, I'm touched. You volunteered your time to teach

those kids about baseball."

"Did I say volunteer? I'm getting paid, but it's not enough to put up with those spoiled kids," Taylor replied.

"Aw, come on, you like it."

"Yeah, there is this one kid, he's got a sweet swing and a good attitude," Taylor smiled and added, "I'd like to pass on what Doc taught me, but I also need to make a living. Someday, I'd like to coach kids that want to be coached."

"Taylor, you're good with kids. You'll make a great father someday." Taylor pulled on the bill of his baseball cap and looked down. Christie broke the uncomfortable silence by pointing and saying, "Taylor, there's Harry. Maybe he knows something."

Taylor drove the dinghy back toward the docks where Harry turned his little boat cleaning side business into a thriving operation with two other divers—not including Taylor, who helped out when he needed quick cash. If Doc's boat was hauled out or moved, Harry would know about it. Harry was getting his boat cleaning equipment in order before plunging in to clean the barnacles off the hull of a Hunter sailboat.

They both yelled his name, but with his wetsuit hood and full-face mask on, Harry didn't hear them. Taylor killed the engine, stood and yelled, "Harry!" Harry turned and waved. Taylor signaled him to wait, he'd be right there. They motored up alongside the sailboat. Christie threw Harry a line and he tied them off.

"Hey, did you arrange to have Doc's boat hauled out or moved?" Taylor asked.

"No. I went to go clean the old boat this morning and it was gone. I couldn't believe my eyes. Where would Doc go? I have a standing order to clean his boat the first Monday of the month. His boat hasn't been painted in so long it needs constant cleaning, you know?" Harry said.

"When was the last time you saw Doc or his boat?" Christie asked.

Harry pulled his hood down and scratched his head and looked toward the now empty slip. "Friday afternoon, as I was leaving."

"Did Doc say anything?" Taylor asked.

"No. Everything seemed fine. I told him to have a good weekend and that I'd see him on Monday. Then on my way out two guys passed me at the gate and asked where Doc Skinner kept his boat. I figured they were fans. I wasn't going to let them in, but they held the gate while I took my tanks out and just let themselves in."

"What did they look like?" Christie and Taylor asked in unison.

Harry scratched the stubble on his face and said, "I don't know. Just two guys."

"Harry, think," Taylor implored.

"I didn't really pay attention. I'm more comfortable with fish, you know. I'm not what you would call a 'people person.'"

Taylor nodded and asked, "Did anyone else see these guys?"

"Nah, it was pretty quiet. Everyone was getting an early start on their weekend. Most of the dock people were aboard the Bottom Feeder. That's where happy hour was on Friday."

"The lawyer's yacht at the end of E-Dock?"

"Right," Harry said, and as if reading Taylor's mind said, "Too far to see anything happening on Doc's boat."

"Harry, would you mind doing me a favor?" Taylor asked.

"Sure, whatever you need."

"Can you haul your gear over to Doc's slip and have a look around underwater?"

"All right. But what am I looking for?"

"I'm not sure, but something's fishy. I know Doc and I know he wouldn't take his boat out alone. He's seventy-one years old, for Christ's sake," Taylor said without thinking.

"Hey, I'm almost seventy," Harry said with a smile.

"Sorry, Harry. But we both know Doc wouldn't take his boat anywhere alone. Not even to have it hauled out. Besides, I've been on a waiting list to have my boat hauled and painted for weeks. Doc would have been planning this for a while and he would have told someone. He certainly would have told you on Friday not to clean his boat on Monday, right?"

"Then where do you think his boat is?" Harry asked.

"I have no idea, but maybe we'll find a clue in the water. It couldn't hurt to look."

"Maybe those two guys stole Doc's boat. It's happened before, you know," Harry said.

"We can't rule anything out, yet," Taylor said as he hopped into his dinghy. "We're going to go over to Ann-Marie's. We'll check back with you a little later to see if you found something."

"Okay, I'll go have a look right now," Harry said as he untied the lines.

CHAPTER SEVEN

"Taylor, why don't we call Doc?" Christie asked as Taylor started the outboard engine.

"His only phone is the one on his boat," Taylor reminded her.

"I thought he was going to get a smart phone."

"You know how Doc is about stuff like that. There's no way. If I didn't get him a VHF radio, he'd still be using a CB. I think he has an old flip phone that he uses for ordering pizza, but otherwise he leaves it off."

"Hey, why don't we try to raise him by radio?"

"Good idea," Taylor replied as he reached into the water-tight box and pulled out his hand-held radio.

"Christie, you drive and I'll work the radio," Taylor said as they switched places. They made their way out of the marina and across the Mission Bay channel, Taylor tried to reach Doc. After they passed the no wake zone, Christie opened up the engine for the short ride to the neighboring bay and Anne-Marie's house.

Over the whine of the outboard engine, Christie yelled, "Anything?"

Taylor just shook his head with a grim look on his face.

Christie avoided the variety of moored crafts and flotillas of party boats anchored in the calm of the lagoon after a warm weekend. Eager to talk to Ann-Marie, Christie zoomed along despite the five-mile-an-hour speed limit. She was careful not to run over any morning swimmers, but she was going a good twenty miles an hour. They approached the beach lined with an eclectic collection of recently renovated million dollar bay-front homes wedged next to the old quaint cottages. In an effort to impress Taylor, Christie goosed the throttle to ride the inflatable up onto the beach but was a little overzealous and hit the shore with a bit too much momentum. Taylor went flying over the bow and onto the sand.

Christie quickly cut the engine and hopped out. Taylor was lying in a crumpled ball on the beach. She ran over to him, cupped his face in her hands and softly said, "Oh no. Taylor, are you okay? Taylor?" but got no reply. "Taylor, I'm so sorry. Please be okay. Please." She reached for his wrist to check for a pulse when he grabbed her arm and rolled her on her back, pinning her wrists. She made a halfhearted effort to break free—which was the last thing she wanted to do.

"I'm fine, no thanks to you. Who taught you how to drive a boat, anyway?"

"You did!" They both laughed as he helped her up from the sand. The moment helped lighten the somber mood. As they walked up the beach, Christie gave Taylor a little punch on the shoulder and he gave her a light shove back.

CHAPTER EIGHT

Upon seeing Ann-Marie's cozy cottage, Christie realized it had been a while since she was last there. It was a classic one-story beach house recently painted canary yellow with white trim and a wood deck facing the beach complete with two perfectly placed powder-blue Adirondack chairs, a small table, and an array of tropical plants and flowers. It was neat as a pin. Unlike the summer rentals, Ann-Marie's house showed a pride of ownership.

"When I finally move off my boat and into a real house, I'd like it to be just like this one. I especially like the idea of showering outside," Taylor said, pointing to the glass enclosed shower around the side of the house.

No wonder he likes the idea, Christie thought. "He spent half his life traveling around on a team bus and staying in dingy hotels with a bunch of other minor leaguers—and the rest on the road with the Padres. After that he went into the Navy and lived in barracks and aboard boats. Then he becomes a live-aboard on a sailboat, not a lot of room there—and showers are a luxury you have to fight for in the marina bathroom.

Taylor walked over to the outdoor shower and opened the door. "Wow, is this something, or what?"

"Yeah, and big enough for two," Christie said without thinking. It didn't matter. Taylor didn't notice, as usual.

"Isn't that Ann-Marie's car?" Taylor asked, pointing to a beat-up little Toyota Corolla parked beside the house. Christie nodded. "Good, she must be home, then."

They stepped over a boogie board and a couple of beach toys on their way to the door. Taylor picked up a tiny baseball glove he'd given to Ann-Marie's six-year-old son, Joey. As he collected the glove and other assorted toys to move them to the side, he said to Christie, "Obviously there's enough room in this kind of a house for a kid, too." Christie smiled to herself as she knocked on the door. It took three rounds of knocking before a weary and grouchy Ann-Marie peeked through the side window and then opened the door.

"Don't you look lovely this morning," Taylor joked, firing off the first shot in the usual good-natured verbal repartee.

Ann-Marie wasted no time in firing back. "At least I didn't sleep on the beach," pointing at the sand caked on Taylor's hat, hair, and shirt.

"Hey, it's not my fault. Christie...."

Ann-Marie cut him off with, "It's just like you to blame it on a woman, Taylor."

Christie broke in, "Ann-Marie, we really need to talk to you."

Ann-Marie motioned Christie inside but put her hand to stop Taylor. In a motherly tone, she said, "You. Go wash off that sand in the shower before you come in my house, mister."

"Okay, mom, if you insist," Taylor said in a mocking tone.

He dropped the toys and almost ran to the shower in his excitement.

Christie's eyes scanned the interior of the beach house. It was decorated appropriately in a nautical by-the-beach theme. There were wood-carved seagulls, driftwood, and seascape paintings all around, with light maple furniture and light blue and yellow walls. It was inexpensive, but tasteful. Christie especially loved the yellow and white kitchen. It seemed to smile and say, "Hello."

"I love your house. It's exactly what Taylor and I want someday," Christie said as Ann-Marie raised an eyebrow.

"I mean, it's… it's… it's what Taylor said he wants. I don't know if he meant with me."

"Still haven't told him how you feel?"

Christie hung her head and answered, "No."

"What are you waiting for? You two belong together. Everyone knows you're in love with him. I'm sure he senses it, too," Ann-Marie said with squeeze of Christie's shoulder.

Now it was Christie's turn to raise an eyebrow.

"Yeah, you're right. He's not that sharp when it comes to that kind of thing, is he?" They both laughed. Just then Taylor walked in, dripping wet.

CHAPTER NINE

"What's so funny? Didn't you ask Ann-Marie about Doc?" he asked loudly.

Christie made a gesture to be quiet.

"Don't worry, there's no need to whisper. Joey's not here," Ann-Marie said. "He's with his schmuck of a father in New Jersey for a few weeks. Part of the divorce agreement. He spends part of his summer vacation with that idiot."

Ann-Marie began explaining how she had to pay for the airfare and never got a dime from the deadbeat dad and started rambling about how much she despised him. If Christie let her go on it could be hours before they were able to talk about Doc. Ann-Marie was blessed and cursed with the gift of gab, but was an equally good listener and remembered everything. That made her everybody's favorite waitress. Christie interrupted Ann-Marie's tirade to ask about Doc.

"We noticed Doc's boat was gone this morning. Do you know where he might have gone?"

"That's funny, "Ann-Marie said, handing each of them a cup of coffee and sitting down on a bar stool.

"What?" Christie asked.

"You know how Doc's a creature of habit, right?"

"Yeah, you can set your watch to his routine," Taylor said.

"That's why I thought it was strange that he didn't come into the bar to watch the Padres game on the big screen TV over the weekend. Whenever there's a home game he's at the stadium, and he's in the cantina watching every road game, sitting there second-guessing the manager, coaches, players, umpires, and even the ground crew." She paused to take a sip of her coffee and Christie snagged the opportunity to cut in before Ann-Marie got going again.

"When was the last time you actually saw Doc?" Christie asked.

"When school lets out, Doc comes over and watches Joey while I work or I take him to Doc's boat. Doc is teaching him about baseball. And the two of them will sometimes go to the baseball card shop together to look at cards and stuff."

"Good," Taylor interjected. "Kids need to learn about America's greatest sport."

"Taylor, please! Between the two of you, we'll never get anywhere. Ann-Marie, go ahead," Christie said, exasperated.

"Like I was saying, Doc had been watching Joey while I work before he went to stay with his dad. Well, the other day, Friday I think it was, I brought Doc lunch from the bar. You know, my little way of saying thanks for keeping an eye on my kid, and he was talking to two guys. Actually, they were talking to him. Doc looked upset. I handed him his lunch and left. He didn't look too pleased, if you ask me."

"What did these guys look like?" Taylor asked.

"Goombas. Like the guys from my neighborhood back

in Jersey."

"You mean they looked like wise guys?" Taylor inquired.

"Exactly."

"Really. What does a wise guy look like?" Christie asked in all seriousness.

"Have you met my ex?"

"No," Christie said.

"Lucky you. These guys were both wearing those nylon jumpsuits or whatever you call them and it's like 100 degrees out. They were both really big with dark hair and lots of jewelry. One of them was short and stocky, the other was tall and stocky. They were both smoking big fat cigars. They kept their backs to me so I really didn't get a look at their faces."

While Ann-Marie was talking, Taylor walked over to the living room and picked up a baseball that must have rolled under a table and examined it closely.

"What is it, Taylor?" Christie asked as she walked over to him.

"Ann-Marie, where did this baseball come from?" Taylor asked.

"Doc gave it to Joey along with a bunch of other, what do you call it?"

"Memorabilia," Taylor mumbled while looking over the ball.

"Why?" Christie wanted to know.

"Because this ball is signed by the entire Mets pitching staff from their World Series year." He showed it to Christie and she rattled off the names, Jon Matlack, Tug McGraw, Tom

Seaver, Jerry Koosman...."

"Is it valuable?" Ann-Marie asked.

"Yes. This is very valuable. Why is it here on the floor?"

"I don't know. Maybe Joey was playing with it." Taylor winced as if in pain.

"Over the past couple of weeks Doc's been giving Joey all kinds of stuff like that. Here, let me show you."

Ann-Marie led them to Joey's room. Taylor looked around. It was a typical seven-year-old's room. Posters of Mike Trout, Bryce Harper, Jose Altuve, and other current stars—plus a signed poster of a young Taylor James.

"Kid's got good taste in hitters," Taylor said as he continued to look around the room. Not every kid has a signed Ted Williams bat, an autographed Willie Mays glove, and a Pete Rose rookie card lying around.

"Is this stuff valuable?" Ann-Marie asked.

"Yes, all but this one," Taylor said as he held up his own baseball card and then turned it over to look at his stats.

Taylor James

Height: 6-4 • Weight: 205 • Bats: L • Throws: R • Born: 1960 • Position: RF

		GM	H	HR	RBI	AVG	SB
1980	Padres	61	41	11	33	.286	10
1981	Padres	147	138	21	81	.311	19
1982	Padres	158	185	31	107	.325	21
1983	Padres	85	81	14	47	.301	12
1984	Mets	53	22	1	7	.190	0
1985	Pirates	17	2	0	0	.120	0

Ann-Marie looked over his shoulder and said, "Should Joey give all the stuff back to Doc?"

"No, of course not. I'm sure Doc wanted him to have it."

"Some of the stuff Doc gave Joey he took with him to his father's."

"Ann-Marie, will you ask around in your discreet way and see if Doc gave any more of his stuff away—and ask Joey to tell you what other things Doc gave him. Write it down, okay?"

"Do you think something bad has happened to Doc?"

"It's starting to look that way," Taylor said.

CHAPTER TEN

On the way back to the marina, Christie let Taylor drive the boat. As they entered the harbor Taylor made an abrupt right turn, nearly causing Christie to fall overboard.

"Hey, I said I was sorry about the beach thing," Christie said.

"I have an idea. Let's go talk to Frank at the Harbor Patrol office and tell him what's going on."

"What is going on, Taylor?"

"I'm not sure."

As they approached the dock in front of the tower, Taylor maneuvered around the patrol boats. A young, friendly, and eager lifeguard met them and helped them tie up. He smiled as he assisted Christie out of the dinghy. When she stood on the docks she towered over him and his smile quickly disappeared. It was something Christie was used to.

"Is Frank in?" Taylor asked, stepping out of the boat, and an even more imposing figure than Christie.

"Uh, yeah, he's up in the tower," the lifeguard said.

Frank was waiting for them at the top of the ramp as they approached. "Hey, buddy, how ya been?" Frank said as they shook hands. "And who is this lovely lady?"

Before Taylor could answer, Christie introduced herself. "Christie Hollingsworth," she said and held out her hand.

Instant recognition crossed Frank's face. "Chief Hollingsworth's daughter?"

"Yup. How do you and Taylor know each other?" Christie asked.

"Frank and I went to boot camp together," Taylor replied, "but he got out after four years and got this cushy job." The two Navy buddies grinned as Taylor continued. "Frank here is kinda famous. He's been featured in a bunch of reality shows and appeared in *Baywatch*, the show, not the movie."

"Really," Christie said.

"Oh yeah," Taylor continued, "Frank isn't one to brag, but he's saved more swimmers than any lifeguard in the city. You're looking at a living legend."

Frank bowed for them and said, "Enough already. What can I do for you two?"

"Were you working this weekend?" Taylor asked.

"Unfortunately, why?"

"Do you know Doc Skinner? He owns a fifty-four-foot Bertram. It's brown and tan with a brown canvas top and a Padres NL West Champions flag flying off the top."

"Nope."

"Do you guys keep a log of the boats that come in and out of the harbor?"

"Only if something looks suspicious or unusual. What's this all about, Taylor?" Frank asked with a more professional tone.

"So you wouldn't have noticed if a boat left late at night?"

"Now that would be suspicious, wouldn't it?" Frank said as he winked at Christie.

"Were you working the tower on either of the past two nights?"

"Nah, I was on patrol, working with the DEA and immigration on a couple of smuggling busts. But we can check the log, if you like. What's this all about?"

Christie spoke up, "Doc's boat isn't in its slip."

"So?" Frank asked, not making the connection.

"In all the years we've known Doc, he's never taken his boat out by himself, not once. I'm not even sure if it runs," Taylor pointed out.

"He's a good friend and we're concerned something may have happened to him," Christie added.

"A lot of boats have been stolen from the marina lately and used for smuggling. A fifty-four-footer would be useful in that regard," Frank informed them.

"Frank, I don't think it was stolen," Taylor said with conviction.

"Maybe it's in the yard for repairs."

"I'll check, but I doubt it," Taylor said.

"I'll save you the trouble. Let's go up to the tower. From there, you can see into the Bristol Boat Yard with binoculars," Frank said as he turned and headed up the stairs, motioning for them to follow. As they made their way up to the tower, nearly all the men on duty stopped in their tracks when they saw Christie approach. She was oblivious, completely unaware of her attractiveness.

"What's the name of the boat?" Frank asked as he picked up a pair of binoculars.

"*The Splendid Splinter*," Taylor answered as Frank scanned the boat yard.

"*The Splendid Splinter*?" Frank repeated as he put the binoculars down.

"Yeah, why? Does it ring a bell?" Taylor asked as he picked up the binoculars and checked the boat yard. Nothing. He looked at Christie and shook his head, letting her know the boat wasn't there while Frank walked to the other side of the tower.

"When I came on Saturday morning, the graveyard guy told me they received a distress signal from someone in a sinking vessel. I think he said the name of the boat was *The Splendid Splinter*."

CHAPTER ELEVEN

Christie was stunned and sat down. Taylor also was in shock. Frank continued.

"That's all he said. 'Mayday, this is *The Splendid Splinter* and I am going down,' then the transmission got garbled."

"Were you able to trace the signal?" Christie asked.

"I'm not sure. The officer thought it might have been a prank because all he heard after that was clicking, like someone pushing the talk button, just not saying anything."

"Do you have a tape of the transmission?" an anxious Christie asked.

"As a matter of fact, we do," Frank said. He found it and cued it up.

After listening to it several times, Christie spoke first. "That's Doc! I would know his voice anywhere. He... he..." Christie tried to hold back the emotion, but her eyes welled up with tears anyway. Taylor put his arm around her to comfort her.

"Frank, that's no hoax. I know Doc, and he sounds like he's in trouble."

Another officer walked into the tower, heard what was going on and interrupted. He looked at Taylor and asked,

"What did this guy's boat look like?"

Taylor described it in detail.

Now addressing Frank, the officer said, "Sir, I think I saw a boat fitting that description heading out around midnight on Friday. They didn't have any running lights on, which I thought looked suspicious. Through the night goggles I saw two guys on the flying bridge. They didn't look like seasoned boaters, if you know what I mean."

"What did they look like?" Frank asked.

The officer described the same men Harry and Ann-Marie had seen.

"Which night was it again?" Frank asked.

"Friday."

"Why didn't you report it?"

"I did. I logged it in. Here, look." He handed the log to Frank and pointed to the entry. Frank read the entry and then handed it to Taylor while Christie read over his shoulder.

"It says here that the name of the boat was covered up," Christie pointed out. "That's strange, don't you think?"

"It doesn't say which way they headed after leaving the channel. Did you happen to notice?" Taylor asked.

"Yeah, they were heading west, but without running lights it was hard to see much past the channel. I think they started heading south. But I couldn't be sure."

Frank turned to Taylor and asked, "What kind of radio did your friend have?"

"The only one that worked worth a damn was a hand held I gave him for his birthday a couple of years back."

"Why?" Christie asked.

"Well, a hand held radio will only have a range equal to line of sight, at best about 16 miles." Frank walked over to a chart and started mapping out the possibilities. "Let's assume that the two guys driving the boat stole it from your friend. Where would they take it?"

"Mexico," Taylor answered.

"Right. And with all the Coast Guard activity along the coast, if these guys had half a brain they wouldn't have hugged the coast. They would have taken it further out, especially at night to avoid running aground off Point Loma." Frank drew an invisible line with his finger. "My guess, they ran into trouble somewhere around here," as he pointed to a large area off the coast.

Christie was looking at the map and pointed to the Los Coronado Islands. "What about here?"

"That's pushing the radio range. Besides, there's nothing there. Plus, that's in Mexican waters and it can get a little dicey dealing with the Mexican government to get permission to launch a search."

"But Doc could have swum to the island. He could still be alive. You have to try," Christie pleaded.

"I can't search that area without proper clearance from the Mexican Government. That's not to say a private citizen couldn't search there if they so desired. I'll launch a search in the waters off our coast," Frank said.

"Okay, keep me posted," Taylor said as he led Christie out by the arm.

"But Taylor, Doc could still be alive!" Christie said looking back at Frank, who was already on the phone as they left.

"I know. And if he is, we'll find him. When was the last time you dove?"

"I don't know, a few months ago."

"Well, get your gear together. It looks like you're going to be diving again real soon."

CHAPTER TWELVE

By the time they got back to the docks the summer sun was already beating down on them and they were both beginning to sweat. They climbed aboard Taylor's boat which was now like a sauna.

"I'm gonna tell my dad what's happening. He may be able to help," Christie said.

"Good idea," Taylor replied as he grabbed his keys and went topside.

"What are *you* going to do?"

"I'm going to see about getting us a boat."

"What's wrong with your boat?"

"It would take too long to get out there. If Doc swam to shore or was able to get away on his dinghy, let's not keep him waiting."

"Whose boat are you thinking of borrowing?"

"Nicholas Purrington's."

"Oh."

"After you talk to the Chief, will you go see Ann-Marie up at the restaurant and see if she has any new information about Doc? Meet me back here in an hour and be ready to go."

Just then Harry came running down the dock waving

something over his head. "I found these directly under Doc's slip," he said as he held up Doc's glasses.

Christie inspected them. "He could barely see without them."

"I know," Taylor said as he looked at them more closely. "Look, they're cracked."

"This doesn't look good, does it?" Harry said.

"No, Harry, it doesn't. The Harbor Patrol saw Doc's boat leaving late at night with no running lights on. Then they got a distress signal from Doc that *The Splendid Splinter* was taking on water and sinking."

Harry looked at the ground. He knew things looked grim for Doc, but he tried to put a positive spin on it. "Maybe he was able to get to his dinghy before the boat went down."

"That's what we're hoping, Harry. That's what we're hoping." Taylor said and then changed the subject. "Hey, Harry, do you clean Nicholas Purrington's boat?"

"Which one?"

"Oh yeah, he has three boats, doesn't he? Uh, the Donzi."

"Yeah, I clean it, but Ritchie Rich doesn't pay me for months, then he gives me the money he owes me plus a big bonus. What are you gonna do? I'm supposed to clean the Donzi this afternoon."

"Don't bother, Harry," Taylor shouted as he hopped back on his boat and went below to make some calls. "One hour" he called out to Christie and pointed to his Rolex Mariner.

CHAPTER THIRTEEN

Christie called to tell her father the bad news. He said he would call in every marker owed to him to get some action from the San Diego Police. Even though he was retired, he still had some juice within the department. Christie hung up to let her father start getting an investigation underway.

Christie then dug out her dive gear and threw it in a big duffel bag before calling Ann-Marie, who said she would take her break from the restaurant and come down to Christie's boat. Christie took a quick shower and slipped into a one-piece black Jag bathing suit, slid on some khaki shorts and pulled her hair back before rummaging around the small fridge aboard her boat for a quick bite. Just then, she heard a knock on the hull of her boat.

"Ahoy. Christie?" Anne-Marie called out.

"Come on aboard. I'm down here," Christie called back. Ann-Marie hugged her hard and then handed her a Styrofoam box with a sandwich inside. A BLT, Christie's favorite. "Thanks, Ann-Marie. I'm starving."

Ann-Marie sat down on the couch in the salon as Christie filled her in on the latest news between bites of her sandwich. "Did you know that Doc had cancer?" Ann-Marie asked.

Christie just stared at Ann-Marie with her mouth full. She couldn't swallow and she couldn't speak.

CHAPTER FOURTEEN

After his talk with Harry, Taylor had a new sense of urgency. Maybe Harry was right. Doc could have gotten off his boat and made it to land, either by swimming in or using the dinghy. It was possible.

Taylor made two quick calls. One to his friend Dan—"Diver Dan" as he was known to everyone at the marina (nobody knew his actual last name). Diver Dan owned a charter boat, Deep Throat, and it was docked at the next marina over. Taylor briefed him on the situation and asked to borrow four full tanks of air. Dan didn't bother to ask Taylor if he needed any additional equipment. He knew that Taylor's primary role with his unit in the Navy involved a lot of underwater work, so he owned plenty of scuba gear. He delivered the tanks to Taylor's swim step—the back of his boat—within a few minutes of being asked.

Taylor then called his SEAL buddy Bruce and asked to borrow a few special items that could come in handy for the search, and hopefully, a rescue operation. Taylor gathered his gear and set it on the table in the salon. He tried to reach Nicholas by phone, but there was no answer. He decided he would go to Nicky's house and if he had to break in and steal the keys to the Donzi, he would.

Taylor locked up his boat, All Washed Up, named for the headline in the *New York Daily News* after he was released by the Mets, and headed up to the marina parking lot where his Fiat Spyder convertible sat, hoping that today would be the day it started. With that car, you could never tell. He hopped in and turned the key. Nothing. "Dang it!" Grabbing the keys out of the ignition he got out and ripped the cover off his black Yamaha V-Max. He figured he could make it to Nicky's and back in under half an hour. A trip that would take a lot longer in the Fiat, but would have been a whole lot safer considering his helmet was back on the boat. The motorcycle turned right over and he roared out of the parking lot and headed for La Jolla.

CHAPTER FIFTEEN

Christie set her sandwich down, not hungry anymore.

"Cancer? Doc? Oh my God! No. Is it serious?" Christie asked.

"He has liver cancer. His doctor told him it was inoperable," Ann-Marie said with sadness in her voice.

In an almost inaudible voice Christie said, "He never told me." She wasn't exactly sure what she was feeling at that moment. Loss? Anger? Betrayal? Sorrow? Pity? Whatever her exact feelings were, they were not happy ones. Ann-Marie put her arm around her and asked, "You okay?"

Christie got her emotions in check, wiped her eyes and said, "Yeah, I'm all right. But why didn't he tell anyone he was sick?"

"I don't know, honey. The only reason I found out is because he told Ray, the bartender."

"Ray? Why would he tell Ray?"

"Because Ray is terminally ill, too. That's just between us, okay?" Christie nodded solemnly. "Ray was once an ordained minister, if you can believe that. I guess Doc just needed to talk to someone who would understand."

Christie whispered, "I never got to say 'goodbye.'"

CHAPTER SIXTEEN

Taylor raced up Mount Soledad, the warm wind making his eyes water as he glanced at the speedometer. It read 110 miles per hour. Taylor backed off the throttle just a little. It wouldn't do anyone any good if he got a ticket for speeding or worse, he crashed. Besides, Mount Soledad was a dangerous winding road with a posted speed limit of 45. The V-Max is a powerful bike. It basically has a car engine stuck on a motorcycle frame. Good for straightaway speed, not all that great around turns. As he dropped down the other side of the hill, he had a picturesque view of the La Jolla landscape. It was such a perfect day as the sun shimmered off the ocean in the distance, he wished he wasn't racing around trying to find a way to find Doc but instead was heading to Marine Street to do some bodysurfing. He had to focus on the task at hand—get the boat, find Doc. Taylor took note of the wind and water conditions, something that should come in handy in an hour when they began their search for Doc.

Nicky was a trust fund baby who lived in a mansion overlooking the beach. Taylor always said it was a shame that such a putz would own a surfer's dream home located right in front of a world class wave and not even surf. As Taylor pulled up to the front gate, he could see a red Ferrari parked in the driveway.

"Good, the spoiled brat is home." Taylor approached the intercom, surmising that Nicky was probably hung over and had turned off the phone. As he pushed the button to speak, he noticed a dark green Range Rover parked in the open garage. That would be Kathleen's, Nicky's little sister.

"Oh boy!" Taylor said to himself.

Taylor knew Nicky from the marina bar. Nicky liked the fact that Taylor was an ex-ballplayer and had followed him around for a while, trying to buy his friendship. Taylor was polite, but stand-offish. But when it came to Nicky's sister, Kathleen—that was another story.

Kathleen's striking looks helped her get ahead as a newscaster. After stints in several smaller markets, she was hired as an anchor at the number-one TV news station in San Diego. Unlike her brother, who slept till noon and spent the rest of the day at the marina bar, Kathleen had a strong work ethic despite her wealth. Taylor and Kathleen were an item for a while, but Kathleen got bored with him and broke it off. Taylor wasn't used to getting dumped and he took it pretty hard.

Taylor dreaded having to face her again. Especially if she was with another man. Instead of using the intercom, Taylor hopped the low fence and walked up to the door and rang the bell. Kathleen opened the door wearing nothing but a t-shirt. Taylor's stomach did a flip and he was left almost speechless. He managed to stammer, "Uh, hi, Kath. You look, uh, nice."

"Taylor!" she said as she wrapped her arms around his neck and whispered in his ear, "What are you doing here? Did you come to see me?"

Taylor tried to gather himself together and not let Kathleen see how anxious he was seeing her again. "I need to talk to Nicky. It's urgent."

Kathleen moved her arms from around his neck and patted him on the chest. "Come in, come in. I'll go wake him up."

"Thanks," Taylor said as he stepped inside and shut the door as he watched her walk away. She was possibly the most beautiful woman he had ever known.

She turned, looked back, smiled and said, "You look good, Taylor."

He just stared at her, remembering the things she had done to him of a personal nature and he shuddered. "Focus," he thought. "Gotta focus." Taylor looked around and admired the handsome decorations. It had to have been done by an interior designer. Money actually can buy class, he surmised.

A rumpled Nicky stumbled out of the back bedroom of the house and yelled, "Maria! Coffee!" and instantly a maid appeared with a large mug of piping hot coffee. He saw Taylor and cried out, "T.J.! Hiya buddy. How ya doin'?"

"Look, Nicky, I don't have time for chit chat. I need a favor."

"Sure, how much do you need?"

They stood in the entry way to the mansion which had a clear unobstructed view of the ocean. Taylor was a good foot taller than Nicky, and he used this advantage to intimidate him. "I don't need money. I need to borrow your boat."

"What's wrong with yours?"

"Nothing. I need something faster." Taylor tried to keep the disdain out of his voice, but he couldn't hide his impatience. "Doc's in trouble, and every little bit of time we can save may be important. I need to borrow your Donzi."

"What does this have to do with Doc?"

"Everything, but I don't have time to explain."

Kathleen stood by listening and taking it all in. Taylor tried not to stare at the most beautiful woman he had ever dated and who was no more than a couple of feet from him, but he couldn't help himself.

"Taylor. Yo, Taylor! I want to show you something," Nicky said as he motioned toward the living room, his silk bathrobe trailing behind him as he walked in bare feet across the marble floor.

"Look, I really don't have time to mess around here. I need to get back to the marina as soon as possible."

"No, this concerns Doc." On the dining room table was a big box. "Look inside," Nicky beamed. "Go ahead."

Taylor leaned forward and opened the box while Kathleen pressed herself against his back and looked over his shoulder. "Focus!" he reminded himself. Inside the box were some of Doc's most prized possessions—bats, balls, gloves and other signed baseball memorabilia he'd been collecting over the years. "Where did you get this?"

"I bought it off Doc. He's been hawking a lot of his stuff lately," Nicky said as Taylor rummaged through the memorabilia. "I paid Doc top dollar for this and the other stuff in my garage. I was just tryin' to help him out, okay?"

"You're a real prince, Nicky."

"I think he's having money problems. He would never ask for money directly. You know Doc. Selling this stuff is his way of asking for help. I'm just going to hold it for him and when he gets back on his feet I'll give it back. Doc is my friend. If he doesn't want it back I'll donate it to the Hall of Champions."

Taylor was stunned. Doc having money problems? Why didn't he come to me?

"Taylor, I hate to tell you this, but I think Doc has a gambling problem."

"No. No way. You're wrong, Nicky. Not Doc."

"Oh yeah? Then how do you explain some of the characters Doc's been hanging around with lately? Not your most upstanding citizens, if you know what I mean."

"No, what do you mean?"

"I saw him with some guys that look like they're extras on the Sopranos."

"Nicky, I'm gonna level with you. Doc's boat is missing and I need to borrow the Donzi to go look for it. My boat is too slow, as you know."

"Yeah, sure, T.J. I get it. Let me go throw on some trunks and grab the keys."

"Nicky, no offense, but I just need to borrow your boat."

"T.J., Doc's my friend, too. I want to help."

Taylor thought it over for a minute. "All right. You can prep the gear on the way to the Los Coronados Islands."

"What? You want to take my boat to Mexico? Are you crazy? They'll impound it in a minute."

"Not if there is a member of the media on board," Kathleen chimed in. She had already changed and had a backpack slung over her shoulder.

Taylor looked at his watch. "Okay, whatever. Let's get going."

CHAPTER SEVENTEEN

"I'll ride with Taylor," Kathleen announced as she walked over to Taylor's motorcycle.

When it came to Kathleen, he had no willpower. Besides, she still had the helmet he'd given her before the breakup and was already tightening the chin strap. Taylor started his bike, waited for Kat to hold on, and then peeled out. Taylor was in a hurry, yes, but he was also showing off with Kathleen's arms wrapped tightly around his chest, which was a good thing considering the acceleration of the V-Max. They made it back to the marina in record time. A full five minutes later, Nicky pulled up in his Ferrari, a fast car but no match for Taylor's motorcycle.

Taylor and Kathleen made their way down the docks and boarded Taylor's boat. "Taylor, has anyone told you this place looks like a locker room... for a baseball team?"

"Thanks, Kat. I like leaving my stuff out. It makes me more comfortable," Taylor said as he got his gear together.

Kathleen made her way forward, picking things up and making neat piles as she went. She laid back on his bed propped up on her elbows. "We had a lot of fun in here, didn't we, Taylor?"

Taylor leaned in. "Yes we did, until you dumped me."

"Aw, come on Taylor. I didn't exactly dump you."

"Really, what would you call it, then?"

"We just went our separate ways. Are you still mad at me?"

"Let's just say I don't watch the nightly news on your station anymore." Taylor climbed on the bed and reached over her, tempted to kiss her, except he had more important things to do right now. She put her arms around his neck while he reached behind her and pulled out what he was looking for, his Heckler & Koch 45-caliber pistol and clips. He stuffed it in his pants, which prompted Kathleen to say, "Are you happy to see me or is that a gun in your pocket?"

"Cute," he said as he pulled away. "Kathleen, will you grab that box of ammo inside the top drawer, please?"

She brought the box of bullets to him but pulled it away when he reached for it and pressed up against him. Taylor felt his willpower waning, but his friend and coach were far more important, so he pressed on—with some minor regrets.

CHAPTER EIGHTEEN

Christie hopped aboard Taylor's boat and quickly made her way into the cabin. Her heart sank and her stomach turned when she saw Taylor and Kathleen together. She wanted to say something but nothing came out. She just stood there, swallowing hard.

Taylor looked at her for a long time before speaking. "Christie, you remember Kathleen, don't you?" Christie just stared at Taylor with Kathleen hanging all over him. She was disgusted and angry. Kathleen was all wrong for him. She dumped him and broke his heart and he was still interested in her? Kathleen walked over to Christie and put out her hand. Christie scowled at Taylor while she shook the newscaster's hand. Between clenched teeth she asked, "Are you ready to go?"

"Just a minute."

"I ran into Nicky. He's gassing up his boat. He wants us to meet him at the fuel dock," Christie said, wanting to split the two of them up.

Taylor grabbed his gear bag, ready to go.

"Taylor, can I talk to you for a minute?" Christie asked.

Sensing she wasn't wanted, Kathleen excused herself and headed for the fuel dock where her brother was waiting. "I'll tell Nick you're on the way."

"We'll be right there," Taylor said as he watched Kathleen walk away as if he were in some kind of trance.

Trying to break the spell, Christie interrupted. "Did you know that Doc has inoperable liver cancer?"

Taylor took one long last look at Kathleen and sighed. It was like he was taking a big swig from a soda. "What did you say?" he asked.

"I said, Doc has cancer—it's terminal."

That got Taylor's attention. "Doc has cancer? What? You sure?"

"That's what Ann-Marie said."

"He told Ann-Marie and he didn't tell us?"

"Well, actually he told Ray one night at the bar and it got back to Ann-Marie."

Taylor just shook his head.

"Taylor, do you think Doc took his own life by sinking his boat?"

"Absolutely not! No way Doc would ever do that."

Christie started to cry. At first the tears streamed down her face, but all of a sudden the floodgates opened and she sobbed uncontrollably. She was upset because Doc was missing, but also because everything was so frustrating with Taylor. He put his gear bag down and held her. Christie was a tough cookie and not one to show emotion like this. But she had reached her breaking point.

"Taylor, there's something else I have to tell you. I... I... Lo..." Just then Nicky pulled up alongside and revved the massive engines of his competition-quality speedboat. Christie quickly collected herself and wiped away her tears.

Taylor looked at her like a big brother would look at his little sister who had just skinned her knee. "You gonna be okay?"

She grabbed her gear bag and yelled over the engine noise, "Yeah, let's go get Doc."

"That's more like it," Taylor yelled back. He caught her eyes and stared at her for a long time.

She wanted to yell, "Taylor, I love you!" but Nicky yelled over the roar of the sound of the two powerful inboard/outboard Mercury engines, "Come on, let's go!" They climbed onto the bow of the boat and handed Nicky their gear and hopped aboard. Taylor went right to the controls of the "Compensator" with a fierce determination. Nicky started to protest but realized it was fruitless. Christie had already taken up the co-pilot position, much to the consternation of Kathleen who was now seated in the back of the boat with her brother. They looked at each other and shrugged.

"Christie, try to raise Frank on the radio and see how their search is going. Tell him where we're heading."

"Won't he try to stop us?" Christie asked as she turned the radio to the frequency Frank told them to use.

"I know Frank. He'd help us if he could. Besides, the lifeguards don't have a boat that could catch us in this." With that he grinned and gunned the throttle and blew through the five-mile-an-hour-zone in front of the lifeguard tower, plastering everyone to their seats. In a fraction of the time it usually takes to get out of the harbor, they were heading south toward Mexico and the Los Coronados Islands. Taylor scanned the gauges. The tanks were topped off. Good. He looked at all the electronics on board as he sped along at over 65 miles per hour. He had to hand it to Nicky. He had good taste in gear. Everything was top-notch including several pieces of equipment that would help them find Doc's boat once they got out there. But first, Taylor had one stop to make along the way—at North Island Naval Station. He needed to pick up a few things that would come in handy during the rescue.

The ocean had a light chop on it but no swell. This would cut a good twenty minutes off their time and make for an easier ride out there.

Christie yelled over the roar of the engine, "Frank says good luck and be careful."

"That's nice. What about their search? Anything?"

"No," Christie yelled back.

"Good," Taylor said with a grin.

"What are you grinning at?" Christie yelled back.

"Frank's search proved where Doc isn't. That narrows it down, doesn't it?"

"I guess," Christie said as she shrugged her shoulders.

They hugged the coast, staying inside of the kelp beds but outside of the surf zone. They passed all the usual landmarks faster than usual as they sped past Sunset Cliffs and the Naval Intelligence buildings. It was an exhilarating feeling going this fast considering Christie's sailboat topped out at about eight knots, and his boat maybe got to 18 mph, before it blew a gasket. When they passed the old lighthouse—and his favorite surf spot, Dolphin tanks (accessible only by boat), Taylor turned and headed into San Diego Bay, zipping by Ralph's, another of his favorite breaks.

Across from the Submarine base were several unused docks that could accommodate large ships, but also made a good drop site for the goodies the guys at the Navy Seal Team should have left for him. Taylor idled up to the massive docks at Naval Air Station North Island and spotted the marker discreetly tied around a piling. Taylor had Christie take the controls of the Donzi and he quickly pulled off his shirt, pulled on his mask and jumped into the water to retrieve the gear bag just below the surface.

As he dove down he was startled to see Darko waiting for him about five feet under water with his rebreather on, leaving no tell-tale bubbles like regular divers do. Darko silently signaled Taylor with his usual "Go suck an egg" greeting and handed him the gear and swam off. Taylor, being a reserve member of the Navy's Mobile Diving Salvage Unit (MDSU) meant he worked closely with the SEALs and they were "brothers" who would help each other, no questions asked, no matter what the consequences.

Taylor surfaced and passed the gear to Nicky who was leaning over the side. Nobody on the boat knew that another diver was down there, and that's what makes the SEALs so deadly—their stealthiness. Taylor climbed aboard, started the engines, and pointed the speedboat at the three dots on the horizon which were the Los Coronados Islands.

CHAPTER NINETEEN

Soon those dots loomed larger, looking more like the islands they were. The Los Coronados Islands aren't much more than barren mounds that rise a few hundred feet out of the water. The main island had once housed a casino, but that failed venture had long been abandoned. The islands teemed with sea life, including hundreds of seals and sea lions. As they approached the islands, Taylor backed off the throttles and Christie scanned the clear water with binoculars to try and spot Doc's boat or, as seemed more likely, floating debris. Nicky and Kathleen made their way to the front of the boat, squinting to see anything that might be a boat of parts of a boat. Kathleen stood directly next to Taylor and held onto his arm for balance, brushing up against him with each bump in the boat. Taylor was so focused on finding Doc he didn't even notice.

They had completed a sweep of the two smaller islands and were now circling the last and largest of the three islands when Christie held up her hand and shouted, "Stop! I think I see something." She passed the binoculars to Taylor and pointed to a spot along the rocky shore inside the lagoon facing west. "See it?" she asked.

"It's one of Doc's throw cushions. Damn," Taylor said as he passed the binoculars to Nicky. Nicky found the cushion with the binoculars and asked, "How can you be sure it's Doc's?"

Christie answered, "See the Padres logo? Has to be Doc's."

Nicky kept scanning the shoreline for more debris that might have come from Doc's boat while Taylor tried to gauge the wind and currents to determine just where Doc's boat may have gone down.

"Taylor, have a look at this," Nicky said as he passed the binoculars. Sure enough, there were other remnants from Doc's boat that had washed ashore. Taylor's heart was heavy. He clung to the hope that Doc may have made it to shore.

"Christie, Doc might be somewhere on that island. I'm going to drop you and Kathleen off to have a look around," Taylor said. The two women looked uneasily at each other. Not only did they not like one another, but the shore was full of seals and sea lions, already barking loudly.

"Nicky and I will do a grid pattern search using the depth gauge and the boat's fish finder to see if we can figure out where Doc's boat went down. Take this two-way radio and let me know the minute you find anything. Okay?" Christie nodded and Taylor maneuvered the boat as close to shore as possible.

Christie didn't hesitate and jumped from the bow onto the rocks. Kathleen hesitated as Taylor tried to get in a little closer. "Jump!" Taylor yelled. Kathleen turned and gave him a dirty look and then did as she was told. The two women started up a path that led to the top of the island.

Taylor looked at Nicky and said, "I think I have a good idea where Doc's boat may be. I need you to monitor the gauges. Look for anything that might be a boat. Got it?"

"No problem," Nicky replied.

It didn't take long. "Stop! Look at that," Nicky yelled as he looked at what was clearly a large object lying on the bottom.

"That's got to be it." Taylor entered the coordinates into the GPS and got on the radio and called Christie. "Anything?"

"Nothing. You?"

"We may have found Doc's boat. Ready to do a little diving?"

"How deep is it?"

"Seventy-five feet."

"What's the water temperature?"

Nicky pushed a button and got a reading. "65 degrees."

Taylor told Christie it was like bath water, but he knew that with thermal climb the temperature could be as low as 50 degrees at 75 feet.

"I'm in," Christie responded into the radio.

"Okay, we'll get the gear set up and pick you two up in ten minutes."

"Got it."

Taylor let the boat drift while they prepared to setup the dive gear. Taylor couldn't help but notice what a beautiful summer day it was. Calm and warm. Sadly, he realized it would soon come to be a day he would always remember as the day Doc died.

CHAPTER TWENTY

Nicky looked dumbfounded as he watched Taylor pull out some of the most advanced dive gear he had ever seen. "What the hell is that?" Nicky asked as he pointed at some of the space-age equipment.

"It's what I use on the weekends," Taylor replied, not wanting to elaborate. "But for a dive like this, I'm not going to use the mixed air. I'll go with standard stuff. Here, you set up Christie's gear," Taylor said as he passed Nicky a tank and duffel bag filled with dive gear.

When Nicky was done, Taylor inspected his work setting up the gear and patted him on the shoulder and said, "Perfect." Nicky beamed like a school kid who just got an "A" on a test.

"Let's go get the girls. Why don't you drive, Nicky?" Who didn't have to be asked twice, besides, it was his boat.

Once the girls were safely on board, Nicky used the GPS to get the boat right over the spot where they had seen what appeared to be Doc's boat. Christie stripped down to her bathing suit and caught Taylor staring. Her bathing suit was designed for comfort when playing beach volleyball which meant it was pretty skimpy. Taylor quickly looked away, but Christie smiled to herself. Then she caught Nicky also staring at her. She gave him a disapproving look and quickly slipped on her wetsuit. Taylor got into his gear and then helped Christie get into hers. He strapped a dive knife onto her leg and two spare air canisters to her BC—a BC stands for buoyancy compensator and is a vest worn by all divers to moderate their depth when under water.

"What's this for?" she asked.

"You never know," Taylor said and then pulled out a spear gun for himself.

Christie looked puzzled. "You never know?" she asked sarcastically.

He pointed at the tip. "It's an exploding head. Just in case we run into the man in the gray suit."

"What?"

"Sharks."

"What kind of sharks?"

"Great Whites," Taylor said, trying to sound nonchalant but knowing this was a real danger in these waters. He gave Christie a quick refresher course in hand signals and outlined his plan for finding the boat. Taylor then instructed Nicky to drop anchor. At 75 feet Nicky didn't have enough line and chain to do the proper scope, but Taylor hoped it would hold. After the boat was semi-secure he attached an extra tank and regulator on a separate chain he found in a hold and dropped them to fifteen feet for their safety stop. Taylor did a last check of Christie's gear and his own before they both rolled backward off the boat and into the crystal clear, but chilly water.

"Taylor, be careful, okay?" Kathleen said as she watched

the two swim to the bow of the boat before they began their descent using the anchor line as a guide. As they descended there were dozens of seals and sea lions coming in to take a closer look. Christie thought they looked adorable. Taylor knew that with seals and sea lions around there are also bound to be sharks. Taylor also noticed as he cleared his ears and descended that the visibility was excellent. That was good. However, as they approached thirty-five feet the water was instantly colder. He wished he'd worn his dry suit after all. He looked over at Christie and flashed an okay sign. She signaled back by wrapping her arms around herself and giving a little shiver. Taylor nodded in agreement and shrugged, smiling with his eyes through his mask. They both returned to clearing their ears and scanning the bottom for Doc's boat.

CHAPTER TWENTY-ONE

Christie saw it first, grabbed Taylor's arm and pointed. He could almost hear her scream through her regulator. They both let go of the anchor line and headed for *The Splendid Splinter*. As they approached, Taylor noticed the gaping hole in the hull. The boat had settled on the bottom in the sand listing to the starboard side. It seemed surreal to see Doc's boat at the bottom of the ocean. Taylor swam directly over the wreck with Christie close behind. Christie noticed air bubbles emanating from inside the boat. She pulled on Taylor's fin and pointed. Taylor knew what she was thinking, that possibly Doc had found an air pocket and was still alive, trapped inside his boat. He also knew better.

Taylor searched for the safest way into the boat. He had boarded it at the marina hundreds of times, but the boat now seemed impenetrable. He tried and failed to open several windows. Using a dive light he peered into the boat, fearing what he might find. When he looked through the forward-most windows he found Doc.

Up until this moment he didn't know what to feel. Now, knowing Doc was dead, he finally felt an emotion, and it was anger.

He could see that Doc was somehow attached to the captain's chair. Someone had to have tied him down. Christie tried to see over his shoulder, but Taylor pushed her away. He grabbed the railing to gain some leverage and kicked in the window. He cleared the broken glass with his knife and swam through. Once in, he turned and signaled for Christie to stop and wait. There was no need for her last memory of Doc to be like this. She protested with some grunting and tried to come in anyway, but using his eyes to convey the seriousness of the situation he made it clear she was to wait outside. She would soon follow him in anyway, but at least he'd tried.

Taylor started looking for clues as to what might have happened. He took Doc's head in his hands and noticed Doc had been beaten badly. He looked at Doc's hands and something struck him as odd. The two World Series rings were missing, but Doc was still wearing the Rolex watch Taylor had given him when he signed a new contract, thanks to Doc's coaching. If robbery was the motive, why leave the watch? Taylor slipped it off and stuck it in his B.C. pocket. He then noticed that in Doc's right hand was the portable radio Taylor had given him on his birthday.

As Taylor carefully examined Doc, he was startled by a muffled shriek and then a thud. Christie had followed him inside the boat and, seeing Doc, had panicked, and bumped her tank as she tried to escape the watery tomb. As she shot out the broken window Taylor tried to grab her by the leg but Christie kicked him away, clearly in a panic. At that moment, Taylor realized it was a bad idea to have brought her along.

When Christie was just eleven, she had found her mother lying motionless in the tub of their Coronado home. Dead of a heart attack. Taylor was concerned that in her current condition Christie might bolt to the surface, which at 75 feet down would be extremely dangerous—maybe even deadly. When Taylor reached the window to go after Christie, he had an anxiety attack of his own.

CHAPTER TWENTY-TWO

Slowly circling the sunken boat was an 18-foot Great White shark. Taylor wiped his hand over the lens of his mask to be sure he was seeing what he thought he was seeing. It seemed surreal. Christie was pinned against the boat, frozen by fear. Judging by the bubbles coming from her regulator, it looked as if she would hyperventilate at any moment. Her eyes followed the shark as it made another pass by the boat. Then her eyes, large and fear stricken met Taylor's as he peered out of the boat's window. Seeing that her breathing was labored, he checked his own air supply. He was down to under 1000 psi. Taylor, an experienced diver, would use less air than Christie, a recreational diver. Normally, at this point you would begin thinking about surfacing from a dive, but with an enormous Great White in the water, you stayed put.

Since making a break for it was out of the question, Taylor reviewed his options. He had been trained to deal with situations like this. He saw the shark coming around again, this time a little closer than before. Don't panic, he said to himself. When playing baseball he had faced Nolan Ryan in the bottom of the ninth with two outs and had come through. In his military training he had been put in situations similar to this—and he came through okay then, too.

He began to formulate a plan. Step one, get Christie in the boat and begin to buddy breathe. He wasn't sure what step two was, but without achieving step one, no further steps would be necessary.

He decided that there was only one way to get Christie into the boat—he would have to go out and get her. She was just out of reach, frozen with her back against the boat. He needed to distract the shark so he could reach her without having the shark turn on him. He made a split second decision, one hoped he wouldn't regret—but a decision he hoped would allow him to live long enough to second guess himself.

He went back into the boat and cut Doc's legs free from the captain's chair with his dive knife. He then slung Doc over his shoulder and headed for the open window. With tears in his eyes he pushed Doc's bloated body out of the window and watched the lifeless form float toward the surface. The shark quickly accelerated and attacked Doc, tearing off his arm with the radio still in his hand and then swimming away as it swallowed it whole.

Taylor watched the scene unfold and thought to himself, "I hope you choke on that radio, you monster."

If the sight of Doc, dead and strapped to a chair, his faced mutilated and his silver hair floating with the surge, wouldn't haunt Christie for the rest of her life, the sight of a man she had known all her life being torn to shreds by a shark might be too much to handle. Taylor pushed the thought aside and pushed on. There would be time to second guess himself later.

When he got to Christie she was clutching her throat and about to bolt to the surface. Taylor knew she was out of air and shook her to get her attention. He looked her directly in the eyes to make sure she didn't do something that could kill them both. He shoved his regulator in her mouth and started guiding her back into the boat. She took a long, deep breath and seemed to calm down before she started flailing her arms and legs, apparently spooked again. Her eyes were the size of ping-pong balls and she was trying the yell and point at something behind him. Taylor turned and saw the Great White shark coming right at them. He shoved Christie through the window and dove in after her, just in the nick of time as the shark came at them, mouth open wide with rows and rows of razor sharp teeth just missing tearing him to shreds.

CHAPTER TWENTY-THREE

Taylor realized he needed to take a breath. He had expelled all the air in his lungs getting the two of them to safety. He pulled off his tank and put it between them, trying to communicate with his eyes and hand signals that he needed to take a breath. Christie was sucking air like there was no tomorrow. She relented and gave him the regulator. He took a deep breath and gave it back. He checked the gauge. Only 500 psi left. Next to nothing at this depth.

He signaled for Christie to stay where she was and to keep his tank and regulator. He pointed to the spare air canisters he had attached to her BC before they began the dive. He gave her the okay sign and she gave it back. Taylor took one more breath from the regulator and began to make his way forward trying to find the air pocket that had been leaking bubbles when they first approached the boat. He knew *The Splendid Splinter* inside and out and quickly located a two-foot air pocket in the forward berth of the boat. He broke the surface just in time. He was close to passing out. He took two breaths, held one and went back to get Christie.

Rule number one is to NEVER hold your breath under water when diving deep and to always let out a little air as you go. Taylor did that as he made his way back to Christie, yet he still felt a little lightheaded. When he got to Christie, she was still breathing from the regulator.

Finally, they had a break. She didn't have to use the spare air which they would need to make a mad dash for the surface later. He locked eyes with her before he grabbed for the regulator. She took one last breath and handed it to him. He only got half a breath as it ran out. He signaled for Christie to follow him as he headed back to the air pocket.

They swam past the salon and galley and into the forward berth. Once the two of them were in the master stateroom, Taylor removed Christie's useless tank and BC and, with his lungs burning, pushed her into the air pocket just as he blacked out.

CHAPTER TWENTY-FOUR

Christie broke through and took a couple of deep breaths. When her breathing normalized she realized Taylor was gone. She took a breath and dove down. He had passed out. It was a strange scene because he was lying on the bed in the master stateroom and looked sound asleep. She knew better. She released his weight belt, grabbed him under his arms and pulled him up, making it to the air pocket without any air to spare.

CHAPTER TWENTY-FIVE

Taylor had drifted off into a dreamlike state. He was out in right field again at "The Murph" where the Padres played before moving to a new stadium. In his dream he could smell the fresh-cut grass mixed with the distinct smell of hotdogs wafting in from the stands. He heard the roar of the capacity crowd as he watched Dave Dravecky in his white, brown, and gold uniform on the mound getting his sign from the catcher, Terry Kennedy.

He saw Doc standing in the dugout signaling him to back up and move toward the line. Dravecky came to set, checked the runners, and then wound up and delivered. Taylor pounded his glove the way he did before every pitch since Little League and chewed on a giant wad of gum.

There was a loud crack of the bat and he turned and tracked the ball to the warning track and timed his leap perfectly. He was in midair about to make a spectacular catch when suddenly he was awake and Christie was kissing him. So he kissed her back. What a wonderful dream, he thought.

CHAPTER TWENTY-SIX

Taylor opened his eyes and she backed off. He was smiling. That bugger. Then he began coughing up water. "What are you smiling about? I thought you were dead! You scared the life out of me," Christie yelled, but laughed at the irony of her statement.

"I... I was having a dream. I was playing ball again and I was about to make a game-saving catch. Then you were kissing me," he replied indignantly.

The truth was, it was on that very same play that Taylor had crashed into the wall and injured his shoulder and his career was, for the most part, over.

After coughing up more water he quickly realized Christie wasn't kissing him but was actually trying to revive him.

"Taylor, are you all right?" He put his hand on her cheek and kissed her on the lips. The kiss sent a tingling feeling through his entire body. Despite the cold, he was warm all over.

Christie opened her eyes slowly and said, "Taylor, I have been waiting for you to do that my whole life." They kissed again, this time a long passionate kiss which ended abruptly when neither could breathe with their masks on. They both laughed at the absurdity of the situation.

"Taylor, I have loved you since the day I met you," Christie said.

"You were only fourteen years old," Taylor replied.

"Well, I'm not fourteen anymore," Christie said as Taylor looked at her with love and lust in his eyes. He was about to say something when a loud noise interrupted them.

"The shark. Oh my God, he's trying to get inside the boat!" Christie screamed. "Taylor, your leg, it's bleeding."

"I must have cut it on something in the boat. The shark must smell the blood and I'll bet it's driving him crazy."

"How are we going to get out of here with that shark waiting for us out there?"

"When you pulled me into the air pocket, did you happen to see my spear gun?"

"No, I don't think so."

"I must have set it down when I untied Doc."

"You found Doc! When? Where? Is he...?" Apparently Christie had blocked out the memory of seeing Doc dead or hadn't seen Taylor push his lifeless body out the window and what happened afterward. Good.

"Christie. He's gone. I'm sorry." Christie stared at him for a long time and then just nodded. Taylor embraced her as she shivered. It could have been due to the cold, but it was more than likely because she was traumatized.

Taylor held her at arm's length and said, "Christie, we have to get out of here. The air in this pocket won't last long. Are you going to be okay?" Again, she just nodded.

CHAPTER TWENTY-SEVEN

"I'm going to go back to look for my spear gun. Stay here. Okay?"

Christie looked at him and said, "No. You're in no condition to go. I'll get it."

Taylor tried to argue but quickly realized it was fruitless.

"Okay, one gun is near the instrument panel on the floor. The other is attached to my tank next to the opening. Be careful." Christie was now full of determination. If they made it through this they would finally be a couple. She wasn't going to fail. She took a deep breath and was gone.

Christie was able to retrieve the spear guns and made it back just in the nick of time, breaking the surface and sucking in a lungful of air. Christie handed Taylor the guns and between breaths said, "Okay, what's the plan?"

"Stay here a minute and I'll be right back," Taylor said as he dove down and retrieved the second spare air canister from Christie's discarded BC. "Okay, first of all, with our bottom time what it is, we are way off the charts for decompression. We have got to make a slow, gradual ascent. Okay?"

Christie nodded and Taylor continued. "We have to make it safely to the tank I tied off the anchor line and stay at fifteen feet as long as we can. We will each take a breath before we leave the air pocket and then use our spare air to make it to the anchor line and slowly work our way up."

"What about the shark?" Christie asked, stating the obvious, clearly concerned.

Taylor handed her one of the spear guns and explained how it worked and told her what to do. Once they got to the anchor line, they would control their climb by holding on to the chain and remain back to back to literally cover each other's butt's in case the shark made a run at them.

"Christie, we only have one shot at this. Let the shark get as close as possible before you shoot him. Got it?"

"How do you know it's a him?"

"Uh, because the shark seems irrationally angry. Something only a dude would do."

"So true, so true."

"Okay, let's go." They each took a mammoth breath and off they went. On their way to the opening each started breathing from their tiny spare-air canisters, which underwater weighed next to nothing and only required one hand—if that—to stay in place while the other gripped the spear gun.

At the opening Taylor poked his head out the window. No sign of the shark. He signaled for Christie to follow him and, not more than a second after they were outside the safety of *The Splendid Splinter*, the Great White reappeared—along with several Blue sharks also hovering overhead.

Next to the enormous White, the Blue sharks looked almost harmless. Christie and Taylor were forced to back up against the boat as the Great White made a pass not more than four feet in front of them. The problem was, without weight belts they had become buoyant and had to hold themselves in place. The two locked eyes and both nodded. It was now or never. Taylor signaled for them to stay together as they headed for the anchor line twenty yards away. Once they pushed off, they were totally exposed and vulnerable.

Christie grabbed Taylor's free hand and they were off. The Blue sharks kept their distance but the Great White shark charged them, blocking their path to the anchor line. Christie, with adrenaline surging through her veins, fired a shot at the white shark as it closed the distance between them, but she fired too early and the spear missed its mark. It did, however, manage to stop the shark from charging and they made it to the anchor line while the shark circled for another run at them.

They held onto the line, breathing heavily from their spare air tanks while slowly making their way up the line to the tank bobbing fifty feet over their heads. The water was so clear they could see the bottom of the hull and the two props dangling above, it looked so close, but it also seemed miles away with what they were facing between themselves and the safety of the boat above.

Taylor kept an eye on the shark while inching his way up, trying not to beat his bubbles and ascend too quickly. The shark decided enough was enough and charged. Christie nearly peed in her wetsuit when she saw the shark with its jaws wide open and teeth exposed coming straight for them.

Taylor pulled Christie behind him and waited until the shark was almost on top of them before he let the spear go. The tip went right into the shark's open mouth and exploded on impact. All of a sudden there was blood and shark parts all over.

A blue shark came right up between Taylor's legs and snatched a piece of shark meat before swimming away. The other blues began rushing in and a feeding frenzy was beginning to take shape. Taylor decided it was time to bolt for the extra tank to get out of the way of the sharks.

At that moment, Taylor noticed Christie was hanging lifeless in his arms. She had either passed out from the excitement or run out of air. He pulled her along and made his way up to the extra tank, putting the regulator in his mouth and taking a deep breath before giving Christie mouth-to-mouth resuscitation. Her eyes popped open and Taylor knew her first instinct would be to bolt for the surface—which she did. Taylor held her in place until the panic passed.

Taylor used the last of the spare air while Christie breathed deeply from the extra tank. They did an extended safety stop and watched dozens of Blue sharks below them feast on what was left of the White shark before they surfaced.

CHAPTER TWENTY-EIGHT

Once safely back aboard the Donzi, Taylor called Frank and told him where to find Doc's boat. Christie then called her father and told him what they had found. The Chief took the news in stride. He'd been busy, too, and had an idea who kidnapped and killed Doc—and why.

CHAPTER TWENTY-NINE

"Another cup of coffee, Chief?" Ann-Marie asked the retired chief of police who was seated on a bar stool at the breakfast counter in the marina restaurant.

"Sure, one more cup would be nice."

"I think I'll have one, too," Ann-Marie said, and came around the counter to take a seat. With nobody but the two of them there, she could afford to take a break. Plus, the view from this side of the counter was much better, it overlooked the marina.

"I just don't understand," The Chief said, his voice trailing off.

"You knew about Doc's condition, right?"

"Yeah, he told me. Even though he refused treatment, he wasn't ready to go, at least not like this."

"Who is?" Anne-Marie said while the two sat in silence pondering what the last day of Doc's life must have been like.

Ann-Marie broke the silence first. "Before you retired, what would you have done with a case like this?"

"I'd assign it to my two best detectives."

"And now?"

"Well, I guess I'd put myself on the case."

"Okay then, let's roll up our sleeves and begin."

"We?"

"I'm the one who came up with the working theory of what happened, so I'm in. All we have to do is prove it with some good police work."

"Ex-police work, but yes, we need proof, or better yet, locate the people directly responsible for Doc's death."

"Okay, then deputize me," Ann-Marie said, puffing her chest out as if a badge were about to be pinned on her blouse.

"That only happens in the movies. Grab your notes, let's get a booth in back and begin recreating a timeline of Doc's movements before he disappeared."

CHAPTER THIRTY

After several cups of coffee and much discussion, the two believed they knew where Doc was (and wasn't) in the days leading up to his disappearance. Just to be sure, they decided to go back and talk to anyone who said they saw Doc that week. Knowing what they knew now, they had different questions they wanted to ask.

After a quick knock on the Dock Master's door they heard him say, "Come in, it's open."

The two "detectives" said hello and with his back to them Les said, "Give me a minute, I just want to finish this paperwork up and I'll be right with you."

Looking around the room, it was hard to believe it was the office of a dock master—other than a large chart of the slips and some framed photos of the docks being built, there was nothing nautical about it. Instead, taking up much of the room was an elaborate set of train tracks with old locomotives and model buildings, bridges, and backyards—a whole tiny town. On the shelves were model cars and old planes—but no boats or ships. In a glass case in the corner was a collection of antique firearms.

Les turned around and said, "What can I do you for?"

Both Ann-Marie and the Chief said the same thing at the same time, "What happened to your eye?"

"Funny you should ask because in retrospect, it may have something to do with Doc."

"How come we didn't notice it before," Ann-Marie asked.

Les held up his sunglasses as the reason. "I didn't want to talk about it because I can't believe I let those two fat guys get the jump on me."

"What fat guys are you referring to?" The Chief asked.

Les told the story for the first time (at least the true story) about how he got his black eye. Two days before Doc disappeared he observed two obvious non-boaters hanging around the marina. Still, despite their inappropriate attire and stylings, he gave them the benefit of the doubt and surmised they could be guests of one of the big shots on "E-Dock," where the most expensive yachts were moored. So he let it go until he saw them again the next day.

This time, however, he left his office and approached the two men and informed them he was the Doc Master and politely asked if there was something he could help them with. They told him to mind his own business and take a hike. You don't tell the only Doc Master the Island Marina has ever known to take a hike from the very place he helped build over 30 years ago.

Remaining calm, Les reached for his radio to call security when he was sucker punched in the eye. "I didn't see it coming, but I should have," the feisty and proud man said.

"That was a cheap shot, nothing to be ashamed of. I've

seen you manhandle unruly boaters twice your size," The Chief said.

"What happened after they attacked you," Ann-Marie wanted to know.

"They took off, so I followed them."

"Did you see where they went?" The Chief asked.

"Better, I got the make and model of the car, but not the license plate, sorry. The idiots parked in a handicap spot right next to the gate," Les shook his head and handed the Chief a slip of paper with the somewhat helpful information on it. "Unfortunately, our camera system went down a few days ago. They're finally sending someone today to look at it, but obviously it's too late to help us."

Instead, Ann-Marie described the men she saw looking for Doc earlier and sure enough, it was the same two guys. "Do you remember if they had an East Coast accent?"

"Oh yeah, they talked like they were straight out of a mobster movie. Definitely New York or New Jersey."

Ann-Marie and the Chief exchanged a knowing glance. This confirmed one of their suspicions.

CHAPTER THIRTY-ONE

The next stop was to talk to Harry again. They found him sitting on a dock box eating his lunch, a sardine sandwich and a banana. Harry still had his wetsuit on with his hood pulled down, his tank and tools by his side.

"Hi guys, want some coffee?" Harry asked as he poured some from his Thermos into the lid which also served as a cup.

"Thanks, but no. We've both had too much coffee already today. What we need is information," the Chief said.

"Shoot," Harry said, and put his coffee down. "Before we begin, I have something to show you." Harry reached over and pulled a set of keys out of his toolbox. "I found these on my second underwater search of Doc's empty slip, this time using a dive light. I missed the keys the first time because they were off to the side, not directly under where his boat would have been—like someone had tossed them overboard instead of accidentally dropping them."

Ann-Marie looked closely at the keys, none of them looked familiar.

"I know what the keys are for," Harry announced between bites of his banana.

"Tell us," the Chief said.

Harry pointed at the small yellow float attached to the key ring and said, "When I first signed up to rent a storage unit across the street to keep my supplies, they gave me the same keychain for paying for three months in advance. The problem is, the printing wore off almost right away, so it's not a great promotional piece."

"So how come Doc's keys sank to the bottom?" Ann-Marie wanted to know.

"He just had too many keys attached."

"That makes sense," The Chief said, now holding the heavy set of keys. "This is great, Harry."

"Is it?" Ann-Marie asked. "There must be twenty keys here, plus there's at least 300 roll-up units over at Bayside Storage."

Harry smiled and said, "Then it's a good thing I know which unit was Doc's and what key will work on the lock."

"You do, how?" Ann-Marie asked.

"Chief, what's Doc's favorite number?"

"Nine, Ted Williams uniform number."

"Bingo," Harry said.

CHAPTER THIRTY-TWO

Once they knew the unit number, and Harry explained how everyone was issued the same brand of lock which needed a specific type of key, it was easy to locate and open the unit. What they found was astonishing. There was boxes upon boxes of old and valuable baseball memorabilia. It was looking more and more like Doc was murdered over bats, balls, and baseball cards.

CHAPTER THIRTY-THREE

"What's our next move?" Ann-Marie wanted to know on the short drive back to the marina.

"When we get back, I need to make some calls," the Chief said.

"Me, too."

"Who are you going to call?"

"My son. How about you?"

"Some of my friends who are retired from the force, and if they're not golfing, I've got a job for them to do."

"Which is?"

"Visit all the pawn shops and sports memorabilia dealers in town to see if our suspects tried to sell off some of what they found."

"There's something that's been bugging me, and I want to talk to Joey to see if my suspicion is correct."

Chief Hollingsworth dropped Ann-Marie off at the docks and headed for home to put his plan in place. Ann-Marie sat under a tree and reluctantly dialed a New Jersey number she was all too familiar with.

CHAPTER THIRTY-FOUR

Ann-Marie confirmed her worst fears with one phone call. She found out her son had bragged to his hoodlum father over the phone about some of the priceless baseball cards and autographed bats and balls Doc had shown him, and the wannabe mobster became very interested. Figuring there must be hundreds of thousands of dollar's worth of collectibles, Ann-Marie's ex had apparently called a couple of his West Coast cronies and asked them to steal all of Doc's valuables for a cut of the proceeds.

The problem was, Joey had neglected to tell his dad that Doc kept his most prized possessions in a storage unit next to the marina, and not on his boat. When the goons couldn't find any of the items on the list Ann-Marie's ex had given them, they tried to get Doc to tell them where he kept them. Doc had somehow managed to throw the keys to his storage unit overboard. Unfortunately, the set that started the boat were still in the ignition.

CHAPTER THIRTY-FIVE

The Chief and some of his retired police friends canvassed all the sports memorabilia dealers and pawn shops near the marina to see if anyone fitting the description of the two thugs had come in.

They got a break when one of the clerks said two guys had just left who were trying to unload a bunch of baseball collectibles. The clerk told the two he wasn't authorized to buy anything himself and to come back when the owner was working later that evening.

When the two goons came back (driving the same make and model car Les had previously described) there were several officers waiting to arrest them. After they were charged, both of the killers quickly asked for a deal and rolled on Ann-Marie's ex.

It helped to have the perpetrators in custody—especially Ann-Marie's ex—but Doc was still gone. He died senselessly and painfully, and probably without knowing just how many people loved him and would miss him dearly.

EPILOGUE

Several hundred people showed up to pay their respects at Doc's funeral. Among them were friends from the marina, former ballplayers Doc had coached, and several current players who knew Doc from his frequent visits to the ballpark. The only person missing—who Doc would have loved to be there—was the late Ted Williams, who had passed away a few years earlier.

After Doc was laid to rest, a lawyer contacted both Taylor and Christie to settle Doc's estate. He asked that both be present for the reading of the will.

In his final will and testament Doc referred to Taylor and Christie as his "children" and left his boat (now at the bottom of the ocean), his prized memorabilia collection (mostly still safe), along with a sizable amount of cash for them to split between them.

Knowing he was dying, Doc had decided to sell off some of his collectibles because he knew that Taylor and Christie would never want to part with the possessions for sentimental reasons. He didn't want to burden them with his stuff, so he gave it away to people he cared about, and was in the process of selling off the rest.

Doc also made them both beneficiaries of his life insurance policy and set up a trust for Ann-Marie and her son.

Along with his final wishes, Doc left a private letter for Taylor.

Dear Taylor:

I am dying of cancer. If you are reading this, then I have already gone to the big ballpark in the sky. It's okay, I'll be up there showing God how to hit a curve ball. All joking aside, it has always been difficult for me to put my emotions into words and to tell others how I feel. Taylor, I can't begin to express how much your friendship has meant to me over the years. I have always thought of you as my son. I was proud of you as a player and more proud of you as a person. After your injury I know you were lost. Taylor, it's time for you pass on what you know about the sport we both love so dearly. I am leaving you enough money so that you won't have to work unless you want to. I would be so pleased if you would begin to teach kids what I taught you about hitting, and life.

Your Friend,
"Doc"

P.S. Taylor, I know you care about Christine and will look after her when I am gone. But for God's sake, this girl has been in love with you for ten years. I would be so happy if the two of you would marry and have children of your own. I love you both, and I hope you will have a long and happy life together.

"Taylor, what did Doc write in the letter he left for you?" Christie asked as they sat together on the grass next to the old lighthouse in Point Loma, looking out at the Los Coronados Islands in the distance.

"He wants me to teach kids the art of hitting."

"Are you?"

"Yeah, I am. I'm going to use the money Doc left me to open the Doc Skinner School of Baseball."

"I think that's a great idea, Taylor."

"It's what Doc wanted," Taylor said as he stared at the islands in the distance.

"What else did he want you to do?"

Taylor turned to her and said, "Marry you."

Christie smiled as she admired the sizable engagement ring on her finger. "I see you really took his letter to heart."

AUTHOR'S NOTES

This story began to take shape when someone asked me if I knew who the Padres right-fielder was before Tony Gwynn. Not an easy question, since Gwynn had been a fixture in right field for twenty years. Being the baseball fan I am, I took a couple of guesses before coming to the realization I had no idea. It was Sixto Lezcano, but for the purposes of this story, it's Taylor James.

As for the other cast of characters, a few are loosely derived from people at the marina where I've kept a boat for years.

The character of Harry is based on my late father, who was a "character" in real life, if you know what I mean. My father was a figure down at the docks and did indeed start a boat cleaning business after he "retired." I often went to the marina, not so much to tend to my boat, but more to see my dad, and we would sit on a dock box and (he would) eat sardine sandwiches, and we'd talk about this and that between bottom cleanings.

Doc is loosely based on my neighbor, Ed. When my wife and I were looking to buy a home by the beach, we rode up on our bikes to Redondo Court in Mission Beach and stopped at a house under construction. Right across the court (with just a few feet separating the two properties) was a small beach cottage. Ed had a Dutch door so he could chat with people who passed by. He was leaning on that door when we rode up and wearing a shirt that read, "Too many books, not enough time." Right away I knew this is where I wanted to be. We bought the house and Ed became one of my dearest friends.

Christie is a combination of people—one of which was a volleyball star at San Luis Obispo State, another is a television producer, and lastly, a good friend who passed away last year.

Ann-Marie is based on my absolute favorite bartender and waitress at the marina. We had many heart-to-heart talks and she predates my wife, which is saying something since my wife and I have been together for almost thirty years.

I think if these characters weren't mostly figments of my imagination (or combinations of people I know) we would sit on the flying bridge of a boat somewhere, share a beer, and talk about baseball and Padres right-fielders before Taylor James.

SPECIAL THANKS

I know how corny this sounds, but I mean it when I say, "Thank you" to anyone who has bought (or stolen) one of my books. It's appreciated. I recently was told my books are often checked out but never returned at libraries. I hate to admit it, but I secretly find that fascinating.

In case you didn't know, there is nothing better as an author than having a reader want to talk about the plot, the characters, or the inspiration for a book. It doesn't happen often enough (I'm needy that way) but for those who have taken the time to write, call, or e-mail me about one of my books, I thank you. Even better, when I'm at a party and a reader wants to know this inspiration for this or that, it makes my day.

Speaking of readers, this book has been "crowd edited" (I'm not sure if that's a real term), and I'd like to individually thank each and every one of you who took the time to read and critique this book, starting with Mary Valerio, my go-to for pain and punishment (meaning proper punctuation). Also, Bobbin Beam, Shelby Beckett, Julie Belmont, Arthur Beltran, Diana Chase, Rebecka Durham, Valerie Erwin, Patsy Gonzales, Deborah Gunn, Doug Hall, Jacque Knight, Georgann Koenig, Paul Noriega, Peggy Rew, Garrie Lynn Rhodes, and Phyllis Zakrajsek. Thank you all for taking the time to dot the "t's" and cross the "i's"—you see why I needed you.

Over the years, Andrew Chapman has been my go-to guy for everything publishing related. Once again he came through for me.

Last, but absolutely not least, I want to thank my wife and two sons for allowing me to do what I love—tell stories and write books.

ABOUT THE AUTHOR

Lee Silber is the award-winning author of 23 books, including 18 works of nonfiction, four novels, and one book of short stories. *The Splendid Splinter* first appeared in *Summer Stories*, a collection of Silber's short stories, and some of the characters from the original story were later used in Lee's novels. There was just something about the characters and this story that Lee couldn't let go of—so the story was expanded and the book (or Kindle) in your hand is the result. Much like the ending of this book, it feels like it's finally finished.

Lee lives in Mission Beach, California, with his wife and two sons.

You can contact Lee at: leesilber@leesilber.com

MORE MYSTERIES BY LEE SILBER

RUNAWAY BEST SELLER

Sometimes escaping can be the most dangerous thing to do.

All Kate Ramirez wanted to do was leave her lying, cheating, abusive husband behind and start a new life in a tropical paradise. But that's not so easy to do when he's a well-known pro baseball player being prosecuted for your murder and you unexpectedly become a best-selling author. Suddenly your new, quiet life in the tropics gets very complicated—and extremely dangerous.

Does Kate return to California to bask in the glory of her newfound fame—and free her husband who beat her to within an inch of her life? Or, does she remain in hiding on a remote island living simply and happily and let justice take its course? That decision may not be Kate's to make when a series of events forces the issue as this story races to a surprising conclusion.

Available from Amazon in paperback and Kindle.

THE HOMELESS HERO

In this case, a daughter can save her father and save the day.

Thomas "Big Mac" MacDonald lost everything in the

divorce—his home, his National Football League pension, and his dignity—everything but his prized, classic, VW van. It would be enough to drive anyone to drink, but that's only the half of it. The "residents" of the beach park where Thomas and dozens of other homeless San Diegans sleep in their cars are strangely disappearing at a rapid rate. With the help of his twelve-year-old daughter, Big Mac begins rebuilding his life and clearing his name. But when the two get sucked into solving the mystery surrounding the park, Thomas realizes he has a lot to lose—but he puts it all on the line to do the right thing. If he succeeds, he's a hero. If he fails, he's a footnote—another former football player who died before his time.

Available from Amazon in paperback and Kindle.

SUNSHINE

They say some people have all the fun—Sunshine Blake was one of those people.

When Sunshine was a teenager she made a promise to herself to see the world and live a glamorous life. Nobody believed she could do it. Why would they? She was abused and abandoned by her parents and shuffled from foster home to foster home in the poorest part of the country.

Yet Sunshine accomplished everything she set out to do—and then some. She traveled the world, succeeded in real estate, founded a cosmetics company, hung out with Hollywood's elite, married in Morocco (and later escaped), appeared on television, sang on a country record, lived and explored Europe in a camper van, ran a resort in Fiji, and raised two sons as a single mom.

Sunshine's extraordinary life was a wild and exciting ride with twists and turns, ups and downs, and adventures all over the globe. She lived, she loved, she succeeded, and she failed. Her amazing story holds clues to how we can all live a full life with no regrets, no excuses, and no worries. Sunshine's incredible life story can change yours.

Available from Amazon in paperback and Kindle.

Made in the USA
Las Vegas, NV
13 May 2021

22924219R00075